D1164849

The Key to My Heart

By Nira Harel

Illustrated by Yossi Abulafia

To Yair and to Alon

The Key to My Heart

By Nira Harel

Illustrated by Yossi Abulafia

Kane/Miller

BOOK PUBLISHERS

Jonathan's dad keeps his keys on a key chain.

On the key chain is a picture of Jonathan.

"Why do you have so many keys?" Jonathan always asks.

"Because I have to open so many doors," his dad answers.

"Which doors?"

Dad holds up the keys one by one.

"This is the key to our house,

this is the key to our car,

this is the key to the garage,

this is the key to my office,

this is the key to Grandma's house...

and this is the picture that is more important than any of them."

One day, Jonathan's dad was a little late picking him up from school.

He waited and waited, but no Dad.

Alma's father came, and David's…and then finally!

"Dad!" Jonathan called.

"I'm sorry I'm late."

"That's okay," said Jonathan. "Can we play for a little while?"

They played in the playground until they were both very tired,

and it was time to head <u>home</u>.

The door was locked when they arrived.

"I guess Mom isn't home yet," said Dad. "Can you get the keys out of my bag?"

Jonathan looked through the bag but couldn't find them. Neither could Dad.

"I don't know what could have happened to them," he said.

"Maybe you left them in your office," Jonathan suggested.

"No, I remember locking the door on my way out."

"I went to the post office, I had a slice of pizza,
I bought a newspaper…what else? I had my hair cut. That's it.
Then I picked you up. We need to retrace my steps," Dad said.
And off they went.

Their first stop was the post office.

"Hi Peter," said Jonathan's dad, "I don't suppose you've found my keys?"

"What kind of keys?" asked Peter.

"Five keys on a key chain, with a picture of Jonathan."

"Sorry, haven't seen them," said Peter.

"Would you like a stamp though, young man?" he asked Jonathan.

Jonathan stretched out both hands and got a stamp on each one.

Next they went to the barbershop.

"Did I leave my keys here by any chance?" Dad asked Jack, the barber.

"What do they look like?" asked Jack.

"The key chain has a picture of my son attached."

Jack shook his head. "Sorry. But I do see someone that needs a haircut!"

Jack put Jonathan up on the barber's chair.

"Don't cut it too short," said Jonathan. "I like long hair."

"Don't worry," said Jack.

After the haircut Jonathan was hungry.

"Right," said Dad, "to the pizza parlor."

Jonathan's dad said hello to the cooks in the restaurant.

"Did I leave a set of keys here? A key chain with a picture attached?"

"Haven't seen them," said the cooks. "But how about some pizza?"

"Please," said Jonathan.

"Now, where haven't we been yet?" Dad tried to remember.

"You said you bought a newspaper,"

Jonathan reminded him, and they went to the store.

"What can I help you with, sweetie?" asked the woman in the shop.

"We're looking for my dad's keys," answered Jonathan. "Have you found them?"

"Yes," said the shopkeeper, "I have them right here."

She handed them a set of keys with a tiny soccer ball attached to the key chain.

"Those aren't ours," said Jonathan glumly.

"That's it," said Dad. "Tomorrow I'll just have to have a whole new set of keys made."

"Wait," Jonathan said, "I have an idea. What if they fell out of your pocket while we were on the playground?"

"Good thinking," said Dad. They hurried to the school playground, but the gate was locked. "There's nothing else we can do now," said Dad. "We'd better go home, and if Mom's not there yet, we'll just have to wait outside."

But the door was unlocked. Mom was home! "It's late," she said.

"Where have you been?"

"We've been to lots of different places," said Dad. "I'll tell you about it later."

"You don't need to tell me," Mom said. "I know where you've been."

"Who told you?" asked Jonathan.

His mom smiled.

"Your hair told me that you went to the barber shop.

Your shirt told me that you went to the pizza parlor."

"And where else did we go?" asked Jonathan.

"Your hands say you've been to the post office.

Dad's shoes tell me you spent a lot of time on the playground."

"Mom, you're a detective! But do you know why we went to all those places?"

"Tell me."

"Dad's keys are lost. We've been looking for them."

"You mean these keys?" asked Mom, holding up the missing key chain.

"Where did you find them?" asked Dad and Jonathan together.

"Your teacher found them on the playground and dropped them off."

"But how did she know they were ours?" Jonathan asked.

"By your picture, of course," said Dad, smiling.

"I told you it was more important than the keys."

Jonathan took the keys and held them up one by one.
"This is the key to our house, this is the key to our car,
this is the key to the garage, this is the key to your office,
this is the key to Grandma's house…
and what is the picture for?" asked Jonathan.
Dad laughed. "The picture? That's the key to my heart."

First American Edition 2003 by Kane/Miller Book Publishers
La Jolla, California

Published by arrangement with The Institute for the Translation of Hebrew Literature

Copyright(c) by Zebra Publishing House and by Nira Harel
Illustrated by Yossi Abulafia
All rights reserved

All rights reserved. For information contact:
Kane/Miller Book Publishers
P.O. Box 8515
La Jolla, CA 92038
www.kanemiller.com

Library of Congress Control Number : 2002112321

Printed and bound in Singapore by Tien Wah Press, Pte. Ltd.

1 2 3 4 5 6 7 8 9 10
ISBN 1-929132-40-9